FOREWORD

Baby Says was the first of a series of baby books that my father was working on, but because it was the last book he completed before he passed away, it is quite bittersweet for me.

My father had always been adventurous, wanting to encompass all aspects and formats of children's literature while also experimenting with different mediums and techniques. For example, he used the daughter of one of my aunt's friends, Julia D. Shaw, as the model for the baby in this book. Julia was so inspired by my father that she eventually launched her own career in the literary world.

Since my father's untimely death in 1989, Julia has become one of my good friends. She is also the treasurer for the John Lewis Steptoe Cultural Center, a nonprofit organization founded in 2017, whose mission is to share the legacy and creativity of my father with the world. Julia has always been a fantastic supporter of my father and a great motivator for me. She joins me in my mission to share his contribution with others.

Ironically my father died on August 28, 1989, the due date of what was slated to be the second baby book in this series, *Ella, and Grandpa*. Although my father is no longer physically here, he definitely lives on through me—Bweela, his daughter; Javaka, his son; two granddaughters, Asha and Ayanna, each with their own artistic talents; as well as the many millions of people he touched.

—Bweela Steptoe

JOHN STEPTOE
Baby Says

HARPER
An Imprint of HarperCollinsPublishers

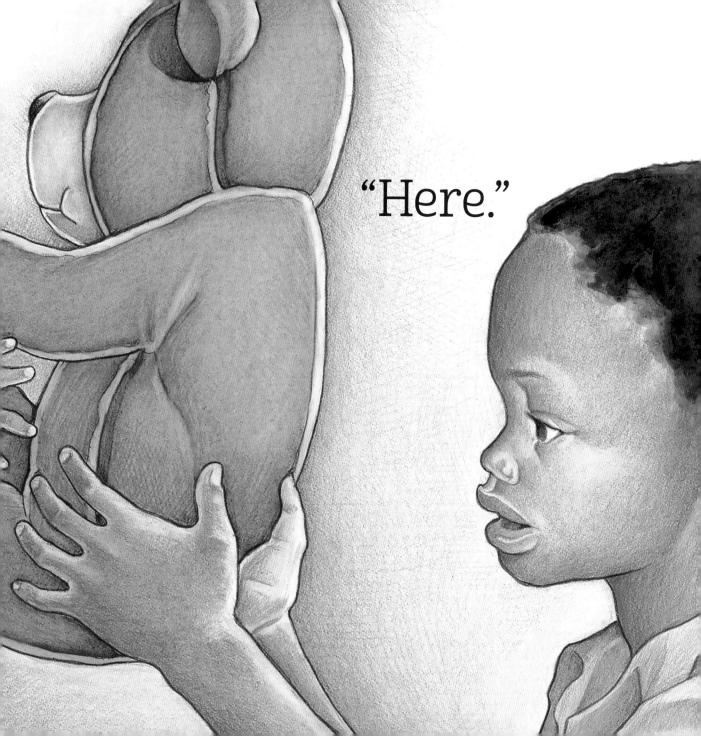

"Here."

"Uh, oh."

"No, no."

"No, no!"

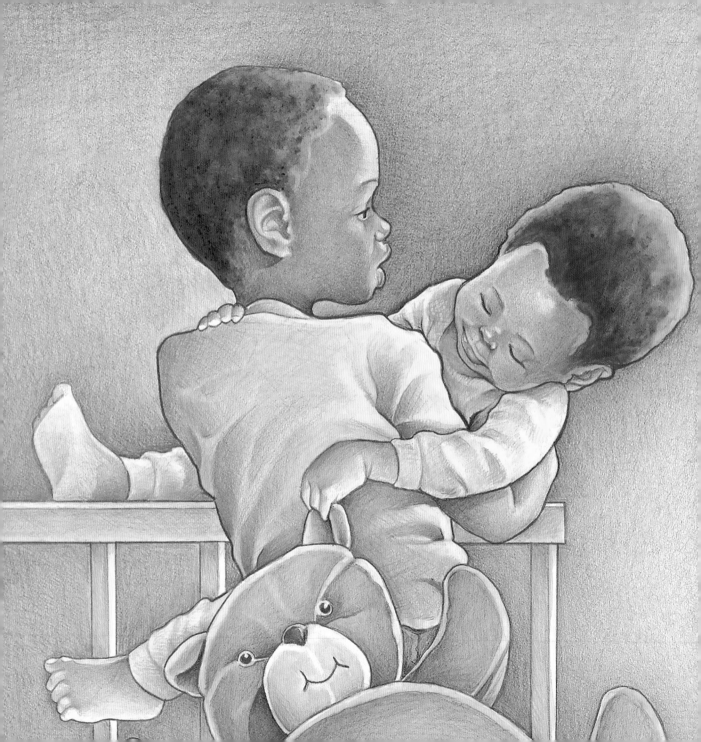

"Okay, okay."

"Okay.
Uh, oh.
No, no."

"Uh, oh.
No, no."

"Okay, baby.
Okay."

Baby says,
"Okay!"

Library of Congress Cataloging-in-Publication Data

Steptoe, John, date. Baby says.

Summary: A baby and big brother figure out how to get along.

[1. Brothers—Fiction. 2. Babies—Fiction.

3. Afro-Americans—Fiction.] I. Title. PZ7.S8367Bab

1988   [E]   87-17296

ISBN 978-0-688-07423-4

Typography by Rachel Zegar

18 19 20 21 22   SCP   10 9 8 7 6 5 4 3 2 1

❖

Revised hardcover edition, 2019.